KOALA
CHRISTMAS

Story by
LISA BASSETT

Pictures by
JENI BASSETT

COBBLEHILL BOOKS
Dutton   New York

Library of Congress Cataloging-in-Publication Data
Bassett, Lisa.
Koala Christmas / story by Lisa Bassett ; pictures by Jeni
Bassett.   p.   cm.
Summary: When Wally and Carrie Koala break their Christmas
tree bulbs and balls, Piper the lorikeet helps them make "magic"
decorations.
ISBN 0-525-65065-2
[1. Koala—Fiction.   2. Brothers and sisters—Fiction.
3. Christmas trees—Fiction.   4. Christmas—Fiction.]
I. Bassett, Jeni, ill.   II. Title.
PZ7.B2933Ko   1991   [E]—dc 20   90-47628   CIP   AC

Published in the United States by Cobblehill Books,
an affiliate of Dutton Children's Books.
a division of Penguin Books USA Inc.
Designed by Mina Greenstein
Printed in Hong Kong
First Edition   10 9 8 7 6 5 4 3 2 1

To our mother—

Jeni and Lisa

ON THE DAY before Christmas, Wally and Carrie Koala got up early and climbed down to the branch where Mother Koala was making breakfast. She gave each little koala some scrambled leaves and eucalyptus juice.

Father Koala looked up from his newspaper. "Are you two ready to decorate the tree?" he asked.

"Yes!" cried Wally and Carrie together.

"There is the box of decorations, but finish your breakfast first."

Wally and Carrie gulped down their leaves and rushed to the box. "You can do the lights," said Wally, "and I will put up the Christmas balls."

"No! I want to do the Christmas balls!" said Carrie.

"I'm older than you," said Wally. "Give me that box."

"Children!" cried Mother. "You sound like two crows. Stop that fighting."

But Carrie pulled on the box, and Wally tried to get it from her.

Suddenly the box slipped from their paws. They watched it tumble down, down, down through the branches and thump onto the ground.

Wally looked at Carrie. Carrie looked at Wally.

The Koala family rushed down to see what had happened to their decorations. They opened the battered box and found shattered lights and broken Christmas balls.

Carrie began to sniffle. "Our decorations," she whimpered. "We won't have any decorations for our tree! All the other koalas will have decorations. Our tree will be ugly, and it is all your fault, Wally!"

"My fault?" cried Wally. "*You* yanked the box out of my paws! I had a Christmas present for you, but now see if you get it!"

"I wouldn't give you a gift if I had to," cried Carrie.

"Koalas, stop this minute," said Father sternly. "Look what comes of your arguing," he said, pointing to the box of broken decorations.

"Yes," said Mother. "You have made your own punishment."

"Oh, we are sorry!" cried Wally and Carrie, and they hugged Mother and Father.

The Koalas sadly climbed back into their tree and sat at the table without saying a word.

"Well, we won't have any decorations," said Mother finally, "but at least I have enough sugar for a big eucalyptus cake."

"Mother, I know you will need lots of leaves," said Wally, nudging Carrie. "We will gather them for you."

"Yes, Mother, let us help," said Carrie, and she tried to smile.

Mother gave the little koalas a basket, and they climbed high in the family tree, picking leaves as they went.

"Hurry!" snapped Wally. "You are the slowest koala around."

"No, I'm not," said Carrie. "Look, Wally, look over there." Carrie was pointing at the next tree. They could see koalas putting up lights and tinsel and shiny decorations.

"I wish—" said Carrie.

"Wishing won't do any good," said Wally. "Come on."
They climbed higher until they came to Piper's house. Piper
was a bright red, green, and yellow lorikeet. He was just
hanging a tiny wreath as Wally and Carrie came to his branch.
"Why such long faces on the day before Christmas?"
asked Piper.

"Oh, Piper!" cried Carrie. "We broke all our Christmas decorations."

"How did you do that?" asked Piper.

"We were fighting," said Wally in a low voice.

"We didn't mean to drop them," said Carrie.

"Well!" said Piper, cocking his head to one side. "I could show you how to *make* decorations. Magic decorations. But you have to work together."

"Piper! Carrie will believe you if you say *magic* decorations. Don't tell her that," cried Wally.

"And why shouldn't she believe me?" asked Piper, ruffling his feathers.

"Piper, how could we make magic decorations? Tell us, please," said Carrie.

"First, you have to get special berries, and I know where to find them." Piper hopped up and down. "Lorikeets love berries!"

"Oh, Wally, we *have* to get those berries," said Carrie.

"Humpf," said Wally. "All right, but first we have to take these leaves to Mother."

They went back down the tree with the basket of leaves and
hurriedly gave them to Mother.

"Oh, I can make a nice big cake with these leaves," said
Mother. "But now where are you going with my basket?"

"It's a surprise!" called Carrie.

Wally and Carrie scrambled down the tree and met Piper. He was waiting for them.

Piper led the two koalas to the berry bushes on the other side of the forest. "Here we are," he said. "Pick as many berries as you can. We will need lots and lots."

The two little koalas filled their basket while Piper chattered and flitted from branch to branch, eating the berries they left behind.

"Now what do we do?" asked Carrie.

"Now we go back home, and you must ask your mother for a needle and some sturdy thread," said Piper.

When they had returned to their tree, Wally hid the basket behind his back, and Carrie asked Mother for a needle and thread.

"What are you going to sew?" asked Mother.

"Wait and see," said Carrie. "It is going to be a Christmas surprise!"

Wally, Carrie, and Piper went up to the tip-top of the tree where nobody would see them. They made a long, long, long string of bright red berries. Piper looked at the little koalas with his twinkling eyes.

"Now hang this on your tree just before you go to sleep tonight," said Piper. "Tomorrow you will have the most beautiful Christmas tree of all the koalas because these are magic decorations."

Carrie clapped her paws. "Oh, Piper, thank you!"

Wally just shook his head, as Piper gave them a wink and flew to a nearby tree. Wally saw him talking to a family of lorikeets. Piper was waving his wings and jumping up and down. Then he flew high above the trees.

"Where could Piper be going now?" thought Wally. "I wonder what he is up to. I wonder if this has something to do with Piper's magic."

That evening the Koala family ate their dinner leaves quietly. Then Mother and Father tucked the children into bed. As soon as they had gone and all was quiet, Wally and Carrie jumped out from under the covers.

"Hush," said Wally. "We want these decorations to be a surprise."

"Yes, a *magic* surprise," whispered Carrie.

They climbed from branch to branch, hanging the string of berries.

"Listen, Carrie, these are just berries. They are not magic," said Wally.

"We will see," said Carrie. "They look pretty, don't they?"

When daylight came, Wally woke up early. "It is Christmas," he thought.

He opened one eye and then the other. He jumped out of bed and rushed to wake up Carrie.

"Look, look!" cried Wally.

The Koala family tree was a dazzling sight. Bright lorikeets were perched on the branches, eating the berries that Wally and Carrie had hung.

"Get out of bed, out of bed!" cried Piper, kicking up his legs and singing at the top of his voice:

A Berry Christmas!
A Merry Christmas!
A Happy Christmas in your tree,
From every bird, including me!

Then the other lorikeets burst into song, and Mother and Father sat up in bed and rubbed their eyes. They stared up through the branches at their dazzling tree.

"Wally! Carrie! Look!" they cried.

The other koala families gathered around the trunk of the tree and blinked at the bright colors.

"What a beautiful Christmas tree!" they cried.

"Come on up," called Father Koala. "Come and share our eucalyptus cake."

The other koalas clambered into the tree.

They all sang Christmas songs with the lorikeets and ate the
Christmas cake.

"Carrie," said Wally, "I have a present for you."

"I have one for you, too," said Carrie. She opened the
present from Wally as he peeked into the package from her.

"Just what I wanted," said Carrie, pulling juicy eucalyptus leaves from the box.

"Yes, how did you know I wanted leaves?" asked Wally, and he began to chuckle. Carrie began to giggle, and soon they were laughing together.

"I don't see any long faces now," said Piper, hopping along the branch beside them.

"This has been the best Christmas ever!" exclaimed Carrie.

"Piper, maybe those decorations really *are* magic," said Wally.

"Maybe? Why look at your family tree. Don't you know magic when it's all around you?" cried Piper, and he gave them a wink.